CALVIN

Written by
JR and Vanessa Ford

Illustrated by
Kayla Harren

putnam

G. P. PUTNAM'S SONS

For the teachers and role models who wrapped
their arms around our family: Myesha Seabron, Maria Nguyen,
Jessica Cisneros, Tyrone Ferrell, Guye Turner, Stacey Dunleavy,
Jennifer Hajj, Amy Fennelly, Emma Quinlan, Gavin Grimm,
Rebecca Kling, and Joanna Cifredo. —J.R.F. and V.F.

For my loving, generous, and supportive parents. —K.H.

G. P. PUTNAM'S SONS • An imprint of Penguin Random House LLC, New York • Text copyright © 2021 by Vanessa Ford and JR Ford
Illustrations copyright © 2021 by Kayla Harren • Penguin supports copyright. Copyright fuels creativity, encourages diverse voices,
promotes free speech, and creates a vibrant culture. Thank you for buying an authorized edition of this book and for complying with copy-
right laws by not reproducing, scanning, or distributing any part of it in any form without permission. You are supporting writers and allowing
Penguin to continue to publish books for every reader. • G. P. Putnam's Sons is a registered trademark of Penguin Random House LLC.
Visit us online at penguinrandomhouse.com • Library of Congress Cataloging-in-Publication Data is available.
Manufactured in China by RR Donnelley Asia Printing Solutions Ltd. • ISBN 9780593108673 • 10 9 8 7 6 5 4 3 2 1 • RRD
Design by Nicole Rheingans • Text set in Casus Pro • The art was done in Adobe Photoshop and Procreate.

For as long as I could remember,
I knew I was a boy.

I'd draw myself with short hair
and a shirt like Papa's.
I'd dream about swim trunks
like my dad and brother wore.

I didn't tell my family until the night before
our summer trip to Gigi and Papa's.
I was scared they wouldn't believe me.
But I knew it was time to be me.

Whenever I have to do something scary,
my dad always says,
"Take deep breaths and count down from five."

Breathe in. Breathe out.

5 - 4 - 3 - 2 - 1 .

"I'm not a girl," I told my family.

"I'm a boy—a boy in my heart and in my brain."

"We love you if you are a girl, boy, neither, or both.
We love you whoever you are," my dad said.
Later, Dad told me the word for how I felt was *transgender*.
Being transgender means other people think you are one
gender, but inside, you know you are a different one.

I wondered how Gigi and Papa would react.
As we got closer, I squeezed my stuffed lion to my chest.
I had already told my family who I was.
Now I needed to tell them my name.

"The same name as your favorite
stuffed lion?" Dad asked.
"It's why I named him that.
It's always been my name to me."

When we got to Gigi and Papa's,
Dad told them my new name.

He introduced *me*.

Our summer trip turned out to be the best ever!
At the comic convention, Papa bought me
my favorite costume. My favorite superhero
signed my poster, using my real name.

At Water World, Gigi bought me and
my brother matching swim trunks.

Even the water slides
felt better in them.

In line for popcorn, I made a new friend.
I felt proud to tell him my name.

We spent the whole day together.

On the last day of vacation, at the big outlet stores near
Gigi and Papa's, I picked out new clothes.

That night, I gave my family a fashion show.
"You look so handsome," Gigi told me.

School was starting soon,
and I knew there was only
one more thing I needed
to feel like me.

When I looked in the mirror,
I finally saw . . .

me.

Dad said there were other transgender people in the world, but I didn't know any kids like me at my school—and school started next week.

Being the only one felt scary.

How would everyone treat me?

What if my friends wouldn't call me "he"?

What if . . . what if . . . what if.

The first day of school, I dragged my feet to the door.

Breathe in. Breathe out.

5 - 4 - 3 - 2 - 1 .

"Welcome back to school!
We're glad you're here!"
When the principal said my name,
I felt safe and happy.

Violet skipped up to me,
calling out my new name, too.
"You know my name?" I asked.

"Yup! Your dad told my mom you're a boy now."
"I've always been a boy inside. Are we still friends?"
"Yes! Did you bring your jump rope for recess?"

When I stepped inside my classroom,
I couldn't believe what I saw.

The cubby.
The lunch chart.
The homework station
and the mailboxes.
The name tag on the table.

My new name was everywhere!
Everywhere it should be.

I felt my fears start to go away.
"Welcome back, class! For morning meeting,
we'll all share about our summers."
I knew just what I would say when it was my turn.

I stood up proudly to share my summer story.

But first, I introduced myself.

"Hi," I said. "My name is Calvin. C-A-L-V-I-N."

And I felt my what-ifs melt away . . .

AUTHORS' NOTE

This book is about a young boy, Calvin, who wants to be seen for who he truly is.

Convincing others that *you* know who you are—and that you know better than anyone else—can be tough for anyone, and can be especially difficult for transgender children.[1] Calvin is transgender, meaning that even though everyone thought he was a girl when he was born, Calvin knew in his heart and in his brain that he was actually a boy. We first learned about transgender identity from one of our children, who we had thought was a boy. She told us, at about Calvin's age, "I'm a girl—a girl in my heart and in my brain."

We also learned that transgender children can thrive when they are supported by their family, friends, and school.[2] In this book, the support Calvin receives is based on existing best practices. Calvin sees his name on his cubby, on the lunch chart, and around the classroom. The principal makes sure to call Calvin by his name. Calvin's friend Violet also knows about Calvin's new name because her parents made sure to tell her. The adults in Calvin's life make it clear they support Calvin in being who he truly is. Affirming and celebrating a transgender child's name and gender is critical to the well-being of that child.[3]

Calvin's experience also mirrors that of our own transgender child and of the many other transgender children who helped inspire this story. We know that talking about these topics with children can be tricky, especially if you're learning about them for the first time, too. That's why we wrote this book, but we could only write it with the help of others.

As advocates, we've been lucky enough to take this journey as parents alongside thousands of others of all ages and genders, which has ultimately made our lives better and our family stronger. Calvin's story is an amalgamation of the experiences we've had with countless trans kids thriving when they're supported by the adults in their lives.[4]

We hope this book provides an example of how brightly transgender children can shine, if they're only given the chance.

—JR and Vanessa
Spring 2021

1. For more information on transgender youth and the hardships they face, visit
    thetrevorproject.org/2019/02/22/research-brief-data-on-transgender-youth/
2. The research backs this up: Support transgender kids, and they do just as well as any other children.
    For more information, visit miamioh.edu/ehs/news/2018/03/transgender-thrive.html
3. For more on working with transgender youth in schools, visit
    hrc.org/resources/schools-in-transition-a-guide-for-supporting-transgender-students-in-k-12-s
4. For more information on teaching young children about gender identity, visit
    plannedparenthood.org/learn/parents/preschool/how-do-i-talk-with-my-preschooler-about-identity